XENA:
All I Need
to Know
I Learned
From the
Warrior
Princess

XENA:
All I Need
to Know
I Learned
From the
Warrior
Princess

Gabrielle,
Bard of Poteidaia

as translated
by Josepha Sherman

POCKET BOOKS
New York   London   Toronto   Sydney   Tokyo   Singapore

An *Original* Publication of POCKET BOOKS

POCKET BOOKS, a division of Simon & Schuster Inc.
1230 Avenue of the Americas, New York, NY 10020

ISBN 978-0-6710-2389-8

First Pocket Books trade paperback printing September 1998

10 9 8 7 6 5 4 3 2

POCKET and colophon are registered trademarks of
Simon & Schuster Inc.

Printed in the U.S.A.

TEN THINGS I'VE LEARNED WHILE PLAYING "GABRIELLE"

1. When in doubt, use a stick.
2. See the world, with comfortable walking shoes.
3. Variety is the key to any wardrobe.
4. The art of negotiating.
5. The best way to overcome raw squid intolerance.
6. How to fight without anyone getting hurt.
7. Only way to keep the peace with a horse, bribe him with treats.
8. Make yourself sound clever by beginning your sentences with, "It's been said . . ."
9. How to assist in surgery.
10. 101 ways to "act" while a knife is placed at your throat.

Renee O'Connor

Los Angeles, California

TRANSLATOR'S INTRODUCTION

By now, everyone has surely heard of the Branson Foundation's recent expeditions to the Greek Isles and the surrounding lands and seen pictures of at least some of the finds, such as the by now famous palace mural that seems to show a leather-clad warrior woman performing a series of acrobatic leaps, with a caption that appears to read, "Yi yi yi yi"—presumably a ritual chant—or the temple vase that appears to be gold but is actually brass with a thin gold plating, which bears the inscription "Salmoneus the Honest."

Then, of course, there are the scrolls, a most astonishing collection, indeed. Some of them are too badly damaged by time or the elements for scholars to be able to make out more than such tantalizing clues as "Our Exclusive Interview with Callist—"

That one ends with what seems to be a bloodstain and a rip made by some manner of sharp implement.

But perhaps the greatest find of the expedition was a collection of scrolls, found by purest chance in almost perfect condition, consisting of a run of several months of *The Athenian Times.*

These long-lost records shine a sharp, fascinating new light into the lives of the people of ancient times. Most of the information they contain will be of interest only to archaeologists and historians. But there is one recurring element, a series of interviews with a traveling bard named Gabrielle.

Amazingly enough, these do appear to be the actual interviews with *the* Gabrielle, the friend and boon companion of the Warrior Princess Xena on her heroic adventures.

Much work has gone into the deciphering of these interviews, a translation of which, it was hoped, might settle many long-standing debates (for instance, was "Joxer" a Buffoon Deity, a Divine Fool, or could he have been an actual man?).

Now that the definitive translation has at last been made, it seems the hope was not in vain. For the answer to the Joxer riddle and many others, let us return now to those thrilling days of yore.

—JOSEPHA SHERMAN

XENA:
All I Need
to Know
I Learned
From the
Warrior
Princess

A Wandering Bard
Gathers No Hearth

Another of the questions I'm always being asked is "What was it like, setting out on the road for the first time?"

The answer, in a word, is—terrifying! Here I was, turning my back on everything I'd known from childhood, everything safe and secure, and setting out into the utter unknown. Of course I was scared!

Why did I do it? I wish I could say something noble and properly bardic, but the true answer is that I'm not really sure. I was bored, yes, restless, certainly, knowing everybody in Poteidaia far, far too well. And Perdicas . . . if I had known then . . .

But neither of us were yet whom we would become, if that makes any sense. And back then, I knew only that I couldn't marry and settle down and be a nice, docile village wife, but was pretty much giving up on figuring out what to do about that.

And then Xena swept into the village like a fresh, clean wind, and the world suddenly opened up for me. I knew only that I couldn't let her get away, because once she was gone, I'd never have the nerve to leave.

So I followed her.

And followed her.

And followed her.

It says a great deal for Xena's patience, and for her determination to stay on the side of Good, that she didn't just kill me. I must have been a thoroughly irritating kid back then. Gabby Gabby, I admit it. But I was talking so much to hide the fact that I was scared silly!

Nothing was easy. I had never slept on the ground before or had to forage for something to eat. I had never gone without a roof over my head, either, or realized just how dangerous it was outside the walls of my village.

But I had also never realized just how beautiful it was out there, either, or how exciting it is never to know what wonders might lie ahead.

Most of all, I had never realized just how close I'd grow to Xena. For she has become my sister not of the body, but of the heart.

"We all eventually become
what we pretend to be."

Xena, "Blind Faith"

LOST AND FOUND

Nerve, that is.

When I first started out on the road with Xena, I had no idea of what I'd find, and no idea at all of just how dangerous life could be for a woman on her own.

I mean, what sort of perils does a woman in a sheltered village face? A pot might boil over and scald you, or you might cut yourself with a paring knife. That's generally as bad as it gets.

But on the road, you never know when you're going to come across bandits who want to rob you (in more than one way), or warlords who want to enslave or kill you. And you can't go running to husband or brother or father. There's just you.

I can't say I've gotten used to it. You never get used to someone trying to kill you. But I'm ready for it now; I can defend myself. More important, I *know* that I can defend myself.

That wasn't always the case. I admit it: once during a confrontation with bandits, I got so scared of what might happen that I ran away, all the way back to my village. It was so terribly comforting to be back with my family, particularly with my sister. I might even have abandoned Xena and gone back to being a nice, peaceful, proper young woman.

But of course I had gone too far for that, even though I didn't realize it at the time. Besides, the world has a way of following you. Poteidaia lay in the path of the warlord Damon, and everyone in the village was too scared to fight. They'd hired Meleager the Mighty—remember him?—to defend them, but Meleager was a drunk.

Why did I take charge? I just didn't have time to be afraid. I only knew that I couldn't let my village be destroyed!

Yes, I managed to get Meleager back on his feet (I thought then that I'd reformed him, but that's another story); yes, we saved Poteidaia.

And, yes, that's when I realized I'd found my nerve again, and that I'd made the right choice when I'd first gone off with Xena. Off I went to face down the brigands—and with Xena's help, I won.

What it all comes down to is simply this:

Try though you may, you just can't run away from yourself.

"You just have to have faith."

Xena, "Lost Mariner"

A Bard in the Hand . . .
Can Talk You Out of
Your Fingers

Well, all right, I'm exaggerating a bit. And I'm
certainly not *that* good—but, hey, that's what bards do,
exaggerate! Or, rather, it's not that we lie, we just brighten
up the truth, turn it into the way it *should* be.

And, if we're clever enough, yes, we can get what we
want without using any weapon other than our voices.

No, I'm not talking about singing off-key or so shrilly
that glass shatters! (That glass-breaking stunt is doable, by
the way, but not advisable if the goblet in question belongs
to the king . . . but that's another matter altogether.) A
bard who's skillful enough can talk her way out of danger
or talk two enemies into friendship.

No, I don't think I could quite manage that enemies-
into-friends bit, not yet. That's downright Bardic Princess
stuff.

But I certainly have talked my way out of danger, and
into it, too, deliberately, I mean, such as during the

adventure with the Black Wolf, when I deliberately got myself arrested. Accomplished it, I might add, with no help from Salmoneus, who just couldn't keep his hands off my tomatoes!

Never mind. He's a nice man underneath that "anything for a dinar" facade, just a little, well, unrealistic.

A bard, by contrast, must never let herself believe her own ruses. There's a little thing called hubris, which is excess pride, and the gods get you for that.

Anyhow, back to how you can save your life using nothing but your wits and voice:

When I was first setting out after Xena, trying to get her to accept me as a comrade, I came across a really, *really* angry Cyclops, raging because Xena, who had, once upon a time, blinded him, had just escaped him again. I wouldn't have had a chance of fighting him. Instead, I convinced the Cyclops that I hated Xena, too, and promised to kill her for him.

Well, yes, I was lucky then, I admit it, more cocky than skillful. But any Cyclops encounter you can walk away from is a good Cyclops encounter.

I went on practicing my bardic craft, on Xena, on Argo, on anyone who would listen. And that, of course, is what it all comes down to, what a bard truly has to do.

How do you get to the Athens City Academy of the Performing Bards? Practice, my friends, practice.

OH, GODS, GIVE ME PATIENCE, AND GIVE IT TO ME RIGHT NOW!

A question that a few careful people have thought to ask me is "How do two people get along together on the road without getting on each other's nerves?"

The answer is—we don't. Not always.

First of all, you have to understand that Xena and I genuinely like each other. "Like," as I'm sure you all know, is a separate thing from "love," and sometimes more difficult to achieve. We do like each other, which means that most of our quarrels are going to blow over.

But of course we do quarrel. We don't always get along. We are, after all, only human.

On second thought, never mind that "only." Even the gods quarrel!

And of course Xena and I have our off days, when nothing goes right and little things start nagging at your temper. You know what I mean: the lacing of a sandal breaks and you can't find a spare, or the fish you've just caught manages to flap its way right back into the water, or Argo has just stepped on your scroll, leaving a hoofprint right in the middle of the parchment, and you just *know* that horse did it on purpose.

And while we're on the subject, don't think that horses don't sulk, because they do. At first she and I didn't quite see eye to eye. I think Argo was jealous of me being there—no, I *know* she was jealous, no matter what Xena says.

In fact, I remember Xena saying something about "sometimes you have to have patience with things that annoy you." And she wasn't telling that to me, she was telling that to Argo!

But it's good advice, no matter who it's aimed at. As long as you can hang on to your patience long enough, the annoying things either go away or else you get used to them and they stop being annoying.

Why am I thinking of Joxer?

Never mind. How do Xena and I deal with our quarrels? Usually by just traveling on. Sooner or later we find that spare sandal thong or catch a fish that doesn't get away. Argo will come up behind me and give me a quick horsey kiss on the cheek with her tongue, as though saying, "I don't mind you, after all." And, bit by bit, everyone's in a better mood.

And now that I think about it, maybe even Joxer isn't so annoying at that . . . well . . . not *quite* so annoying.

FAST FOOD

A good many people don't worship the goddess Demeter of the fruitful fields. By that, I mean, they seem to think that if food doesn't come from a marketplace, it doesn't exist. They're the ones who believe that vegetables actually grow in those neat little piles on a seller's stand, or that the meat you see hanging from racks has nothing to do with the original animals.

"I don't worry about farmers," one woman told me. "I buy my food in the market!"

Uh, right.

Her sort are the people who wonder how it is that Xena and I don't starve to death out there on the road, so far from the marketplace.

Ha! Far from starving, you people who've removed yourself from the real world, Xena and I eat pretty well! In fact, we eat very well, indeed!

At first, of course, this was more due to Xena's hunter-gatherer skills since I was a village gal—"buy food in the market"—myself, but by now, I've gotten pretty good at living off the land, too.

Want to know a typical Xena and Gabrielle meal? All

right, say that we're traveling near a deep enough stream. Xena can easily scoop up a nice, fat carp or two with a couple of quick pounces. Meanwhile, I'm hunting around for some nice veggies, onions, maybe, since they're usually easy to find. I also keep an eye open for whatever else is ripe: berries or fruit or, if it's later in the year, nuts.

Now for preparation. Taking notes? Skin the fish, debone it, slice up the onions, start a fire (flint and steel plus twigs for kindling and dry sticks for steady flames), set our dinner cooking in our (dented, thank you, Xena) frying pan, and there you have it. We usually have some bread left over from our last stop in a village, and maybe a bit of cheese. There's plenty of water for drinking, and berries or nuts for dessert.

And of course, there's plenty of that most essential ingredient: good company.

Can't ask for a better meal.

What to Do with Time on Your Hands

One lesson I learned from Xena I don't think either of us expected to ever learn.

And, no, I'm not talking about being bored. I'm talking about the weird way time seems to have become a fluid thing since I started traveling with Xena.

Blame the gods, of course. Who else but they would decide to, every now and then, unlink a human from the normal progression of the years.

Now, first of all, there was that little matter of the lovers' curse, though I didn't know about that one. Neither, for that matter, did Xena—at first. But she wound up living and reliving the same day several times in a row—apparently seeing either Joxer or me get killed, which couldn't have been much fun for poor Xena or, for that matter, us, whatever we were in that time-loop thing, or even for that never-ending-crowing rooster—until Xena was finally able to put time back where it belonged. It was just a matter of bringing star-crossed lovers back together by stopping the silly young woman who was one-half of the pair from drinking that poison, and getting the two families to more or less make peace. Simple. Hah.

So surely, you think, that has to be the only example of an alteration of time and space that either of us experienced?

Sorry, no.

The weird switch involved Xena again, and . . . well . . . me. A form of me, anyhow. You see, Xena made the mistake of making a wish. Never do that, unless you really want it to be granted! The wish was that she could be back in the days when her brother was still alive.

Aha! The Fates heard, and just like that, we were in a timeline where, yes, her brother was alive, but everything else was fouled up terribly—and I, well, I was a bitter, disillusioned slave girl. Oh, gods, am I glad that wasn't *my* reality! Xena did what she could for that dark, despairing other me and got back to this time frame, which is the right one.

It . . . *is* the right one. Isn't it?

I Did See It Coming

One of the most amazing things about Xena's
many martial skills is that mysterious gift she has for
sensing trouble an instant before it strikes. It's a gift that
she has tried and tried to teach me, too.

More or less successfully.

Less, really.

Xena (helping me up after her sneak attack flattened
me): "It's not magic."

Me (frustrated because I never heard her coming): "Yes,
it is!"

Xena (growing equally frustrated): "Even Argo can do
it."

Me: "Oh, then you're saying that I'm not as clever as a
horse?"

Argo: Superior snort.

But of course the challenge was still there, and of course
I wasn't going to be able to ignore it. Eventually, though,
seeing that if she didn't say something, I was going to get
hurt, Xena admitted that the skill wasn't really something
that could be taught, only sensed.

Sensed, huh? I "sensed" till my senses all ached, did my

best to sneak up on Xena, did my best to stop her from sneaking up on me.

No. It is not easy. Or rather, it would be easy if you were, say, a cat. Or good old superior Argo! It's difficult to put into words. You don't quite listen for the slightest change in the air, you don't quite feel the slightest change in the light . . .

And then came the glorious day when a would-be assassin loosed an arrow at Xena—and I knocked the arrow from the air!

Of course, as she never fails to remind me, I also missed ten others.

But, hey, it's a start!

"Only fools and profiteers ask for war."

Xena, "Hooves and Harlots"

NIGHT FRIGHT

Once a woman maybe a year or two younger than me looked up at me soulfully and asked, "Aren't you ever afraid?"

"Of what?" I asked in return, expecting the usual: getting wounded, getting killed, getting a hundred different nasty fates.

"Of the night," she answered.

And that made me pause. I'm not afraid of the night itself. That's just a natural part of the natural world. Oh, yes, when I camped out under the open sky for the first time and heard all the little night noises without any walls between them and me—you bet I was scared!

I think Xena knew it, too. But she was smart enough to keep quiet and let me work things out for myself.

No, I'm not afraid of the night. Not of the things that creak and squeak and rustle—they're usually tree frogs or crickets. It's the things that suddenly glow *red*, or flash terribly sharp fangs, that alarm me. Those, I can live without.

But there just aren't that many evil beings wandering the night as the stories would have you believe. Or rather, there are just as many evil beings, usually human, who walk by day.

No, what really disturbs me about the night is that time when it's at its darkest and you lie there wide-awake with far too much time to think about all the things that went wrong, and all the things that could still go wrong. The what-ifs. You know: What if Xena had died from that drugged dart Callisto hit her with? What if I hadn't been able to block that assassin's arrow? What if . . .

That's usually when Xena, with that uncanny sixth sense of hers, rolls over in her blankets and mutters something deeply philosophical like, "Stop muttering and go back to sleep, will you?"

And that usually puts everything back into perspective.

THE PEN MAY BE MIGHTIER THAN THE SWORD, BUT IT LOOKS AWFULLY SILLY IN A SCABBARD

The question that I hear the most, right after "What's Xena *really* like?" and "How much do you get paid for writing?"—which is no one's business—is "Where do you get your ideas?"

Why does everyone always ask creative people that one?

In my case, I usually tell them, "Schenectady," which is a small town near Ithaca. But when that doesn't work, I say, with a vague gesture of respect, "From the gods."

Oh, and is that the truth! I got in the way of some godly activities once and wound up with a Gift. Kind of a Gift, anyhow. Anything I put down on that one special parchment came utterly true.

Sounds good, doesn't it? "No more war" or "Happiness for everybody." Sorry, but it wasn't that simple. In fact, that was when I first realized just how careful an author has

XE N A

to be about plot complications. I mean, right from the start, I wrote something about "waking up with a jerk" and yanked our old pal Joxer from whatever the poor guy had been doing and dumped him down beside me. Well, on second thought, I guess Joxer didn't mind that last part too much. He always did have a crush on me. And he's kind of sweet in his own strange way.

But, hey, what about what happened to Xena? I mean, fishing can be fun, but I wouldn't want to have been the fish who got in her way after she found herself compelled to go back to that riverside again and again and again!

And what about those barbarians, riding back and forth over the land? What if I had made one typo? What if, in all that haste, instead of "go to the cave," I'd written "go to the Dave"? Then they would have gone on a wild hunt for someone named Dave, and since that's not exactly a name from any of the lands around here, they would probably have wound up killing a lot of people out of sheer Dave-less frustration.

We won't even go into what nearly happened to the gods . . . I mean, the god of war an ordinary . . . well, not exactly ordinary . . . well, he could never be—let's face it, as a mortal man, Ares is definitely the Guy Your Mother Warned You About. And as for Aphrodite . . . would *you* want to be the one to tell the goddess of love about, uh, personal hygiene?

Oh, and lest you think none of this matters, since you have no intention of writing about heroes and gods, the pen is still mightier than the sword—and just as danger-ous. I'll give you only one example.

I sing here the sad story of Plagerous. Now, Plagerous longed to be a poet. Oh, he dreamed of fame and fortune, he ached to be a bard and hear his name mentioned as One of the Greats.

Unfortunately, Plagerous had no talent at all. Lykos the Baker did. Lykos could bake a loaf of bread to make you weep with joy at the first mouthful—but he could also write poems to make you laugh with joy at their clever rhymes.

Well now, Plagerous thought he could steal those poems of Lykos the Baker and put his own name on them. Unfortunately, the poems were published in Lykos' hometown. Lykos sued Plagerous, and of course the baker won.

The sentence? Plagerous, well, he just had to eat his words.

And parchment, I hear, tastes just terrible!

It's Not the Size of Your Staff That Matters, It's the Way That You Use It

I am often asked if I mind that Xena's got that sword and that chakram, while all I have for a weapon (other than my wits, of course) is my staff.

Well, I admit it, at first I didn't really think it was fair. And I did a fair amount of pestering Xena to teach me swordplay, and of getting angry at her when she refused to let me even handle a sword.

But, hey, after a while, I realized that she had a point. As I got more accustomed to it, I came to realize that a staff, too, has its uses. Think about it. In combat, I can:

Conk a villain over the head;

Rap him on the hands to make him drop his sword;

Get him but good in the pit of the stomach or, ah, farther south;

Knock the legs right out from under him;

Hit him smack on the instep.

Versatile weapon, isn't it?

XENA

And did I mention that the staff also makes a good walking stick, never needs sharpening, and doesn't have to be carried about in a sheath so it won't stick its owner like someone I know . . .

Nope, I don't mind having that staff at all.

"Nothing like a good ambush
to liven things up."

Xena, "The Prodigal"

MY COSTUME MAY BE SCANTY, BUT . . .

People are always asking me why, if Xena goes around in that nifty leather armor, I seem to wind up wearing less and less as we go along.

Well, that's a question I often ask myself. I mean, with all those villains springing out of nowhere to attack us, a girl could use something between her and the edge of that sword, mace, ax, or whatever.

But I've got that something: it's called an instinct for survival. And you can best survive if you're quick on your feet.

If you've ever watched Amazons in motion, you know what I mean. They don't wear all that much, either, except maybe for those weird masks, which are really attractive in a primitive, feathery sort of way but not much use in the way of protection. (They're itchy, too, and during ceremonies they make your face sweaty; take my word for it, but that's a different problem.)

My point is that Amazons really *move*. That's the old

joke, but it's quite true: a moving target really is harder to hit.

And that's the way I do it: move, move, move, and wear your enemy out while he's trying his best to get at you, and all the while you're whacking him in the . . . never-you-mind with your staff. Small, light, and quick beats tall, heavy, and weighed-down-by-armor every time!

Besides, let's face it. Leather armor may look really neat, but it takes a lot of care. Anyone who's ever owned anything made of leather knows how easily it gets scratched up. Needs oiling, too, if it's going to stay supple. And in hot weather, particularly if you're doing a lot of horseback riding, well, leather armor can also really, *really* chafe!

No thanks! As far as I'm concerned, this is one case where less definitely is more!

"My body doesn't make me who I am.
My deeds do."

Xena, "Ten Little Warlords"

WALKING IS GOOD FOR YOU!

Now, here's another question I get asked all the time: How come Xena rides that horse of hers, Argo, while I seem to spend most of my time on foot?

That's a good question.

First of all, we're usually not really in any great hurry. I mean, whether we're tearing about the countryside or just ambling along, trouble still seems to find us pretty well.

Second, walking is good for you. Really. It builds up a girl's figure, makes her supple, keeps off the extra weight—well, you get the point.

Third . . . all right, I admit it. I don't get along all that well with horses. I mean, Argo and I have come to an understanding. I don't try to jump on her back, she doesn't try to kick me. She did bite me once, but that was a mistake; I shouldn't have been hanging on to that carrot so tightly.

But horses are big. If I trip over something in the road and take a tumble, all I have to do is pick myself up again. It's not a big deal. But fall off a horse, and it's a long way down.

Besides . . . well . . . horses smell . . . like horses.

And I don't want to hear from the Centaur Anti-Defamation League, either. You folks know perfectly well what I'm talking about: hot weather, overworked horse—you get the picture. And aroma. Never mind that. It's not just horses. It's other means of transport, too. Particularly, and I write this with a shudder, ships.

I'm not talking about a nice, friendly little boat that you and a Warrior Princess friend can paddle down a river—and even get up a really good speed when you're suddenly being chased by the barbaric Horde.

No. I'm talking about toss-wildly-in-the-waves-and-threaten-to-turn-over ships. I mean, Ulysses was a nice-looking guy, and I guess I might have found him kind of attractive—if I hadn't spent all my time aboard that blasted ship of his being thoroughly seasick!

No. Forget ships. Forget horses. The gods gave us feet for a purpose.

As I say, walking really is good for you.

XENA-PHOBIA DOESN'T MEAN "A FEAR OF WARRIOR PRINCESSES"

As a bard, I make it my point to learn as much as I can of the language of whatever region we happen to be passing through. Sometimes that isn't so easy—we either don't stay long enough in one place, or the locals are more interested in fighting than language lessons.

But even so, there are times when I am really glad I made the effort.

After all, what good is it to say, "Of arms and the man I sing," if the locals think you mean, "Man, arm yourself when I start singing!"

Well, no, that's never actually happened to me.

And, seriously now, there was one time I was truly glad I learned at least a word of another people's language.

You see, Xena and I were being chased by what we then thought were absolutely evil, absolutely nonhuman savages, the Horde. And we wound up trapped in a fort with other folks who felt the same way we did. Scary, thinking there's no way out and that your enemy is something downright soulless.

But . . .

No one's absolutely evil. No one human, anyhow. You may have to look really closely to find that little spark of light, but, hey, it's there. The spark of human light was there in the Horde. Some of them. Many of them. Sure, they could be brutal and even cruel—but so could the folks with whom we were stuck in that fort.

That brings us back to languages, and what a good thing it is to learn as many as you can. You see, if I hadn't realized that the one word I kept hearing over and over from the Horde's wounded, that mysterious *kaltaka*, wasn't a curse or the name of some devil god, but merely their way of saying "water," well, if I hadn't realized that all they were doing was begging for a drink . . .

If I hadn't realized that, well, to put it bluntly, I might not be penning these words now.

NOBODY LIKES A WINER

No, that title isn't a mistake or a typo. I don't mean someone who is lucky at dice, or someone who's always saying things like, "I don't wanna *go* to Athens!"

What I'm talking about here is the drinking sort of wine. Or ale. Or that ghastly fermented mare's milk they drink in the East. I wouldn't blame Argo for kicking anyone who tried milking her!

But I'm digressing. Please understand that I'm not one of those followers of the cult of Prohibitionous. Taverns can be just fine, friendly places where a wanderer can catch up on the latest gossip, and a good many people enjoy a flagon of ale and don't cause any trouble.

But there are some folks who worship Bacchus. Not at all wisely and far too well. Now, there's a devious deity, all the more so because he doesn't seem all that scary—at first.

At first, indeed. Remember Meleager the Mighty. Meleager is a hero, a true hero, a warrior who once saved my hometown, Poteidaia, almost single-handedly. (Well, yes, I played a role in that, too.)

Maybe that should be *"was* a hero." No. *Is.* Even though . . . well . . . Meleager does have a thing about alcohol.

No. Much as I admire, almost revere, the man, I will be blunt: Meleager slid bit by bit into becoming an utter drunk. I thought he'd reformed, and for a while, I guess he had. But the pull of alcohol was just too strong. And he nearly got himself killed because of it. Meleager was accused of murder—and confessed to it because he simply couldn't remember if he'd committed the crime or not! If Xena and I hadn't been able to prove his innocence, that would have meant his death. The death of a truly tragic hero.

See what I mean? Even Ares took to the bottle once, when his sword had been stolen, leaving him pretty much just a mortal man—

Then again, when you're talking about Ares, *just* doesn't enter into it.

But that, as the bards say, is a different story.

BABY-TOSSING IS NOT
A SPORT

I know that it seems just about everyone has found a baby in a basket in a river. Don't worry; your time will probably come along. And when you do find that baby in that basket in that river—hey, you can be pretty sure that said baby is important to someone.

Besides his or her mother, that is!

I mean, you just know that baby is going to turn out to be the heir to the throne, or the prophesied infant who will grow to be the hero who saves the land from a tyrant—it's the way things just have to work out!

That doesn't mean that you should play around with the poor little thing! The prophecy *or* the baby.

Of course, Xena and I, that one time, didn't have much of a choice. King Gregor wasn't really such a bad sort, just scared. It was his general, nasty Nemos, who wanted to kill a poor, defenseless little infant.

And let's face it: when you find yourself with a baby in your arms and warriors start rushing in on all sides, waving swords and spears, you can take a safe guess that they're not coming to say, "Awww, isn't he *cute?*"

That still doesn't mean I liked what came next. I'd much rather see a chakram than a baby go flying! At least the little fellow didn't seem to mind his airborne adventures very much. I'd swear he smiled throughout the whole thing. Of course, when he grows up and inherits King Gregor's throne, I suspect he'll have more than the normal share of flying dreams. And I wonder what he'll make of them.

But then, it's not so surprising the little fellow got tossed about like that.

You know what they say: you can't keep a good prophecy down.

Ambrosia Is Not Part of the Seven Basic Food Groups

Pretty much everyone has heard about ambrosia. It's the food of the gods, after all, the stuff that can transform even a mortal into a deity.

Wondering where you can find yourself some?

Forget that idea. Think a bit. When you come right down to it, who really does want to be a goddess? Sounds good, I know, having everyone afraid of you and obeying your slightest whim . . .

On second thought . . .

No. The problems definitely outweigh the perks. Which one of us can honestly say, "I have no bad side"? And you know that I'm not talking about getting a portrait painted. I'm referring to that dark part in all of us, the impulse that makes you say something nasty about a friend or do something really rotten, like cheating. Or stealing. Or murdering.

Yes, I know, the gods have their off days, too. But do

you really want to see someone like that evil lunatic Callisto sitting up there on Mount Olympus, forcing even the true gods to do her every sick whim? I still don't like to remember that adventure. I mean, what almost happened to Xena . . . I almost lost my dearest friend forever.

I also don't like the idea of any Amazon, even Velasca, going over to the Dark Side so thoroughly, just for the sake of a little immortality—and a lot of evil.

And I definitely hate the idea that I had to team up, even briefly, with that murderess, that utterly evil madwoman! I'm referring to Callisto, of course.

But . . . all's well that, shall we say, falls well. Both of those bad girls literally took a dive. And with any luck at all, mortals won't come across any more ambrosia. No more mortals-turned-immortal.

Besides, there's another downside to the deity business. Think about it:

Gods don't get vacation days. Well, that's not entirely true, just ask Hercules. . . . But I digress.

WAR MAY BE HELL, BUT HE'S GOT GREAT PECS

Some of you may know that I have, all unintentionally, had a few encounters with Ares. That's right, with the god of war himself. And quite a few ladies have asked me what he's really like.

As though I would know!

Now, there are a few rules I can give you to remember when you're talking about the god of war: he may look great in black leather . . . in that tight black leather . . . but . . .

Uh, what was I saying?

Ares. Right.

You have to remember just who and what he is. Good-looking, yes, like the sort of man your mother warned you against—but he *is* the god of war, the fellow who just loves hearing the screams of the dying and smelling the reek of the battlefield.

You get the picture. This is the type of deity who is definitely not going to care very much about playing fair or know anything about showing mercy.

Come to think of it, I don't know if Ares even *understands* the concept of mercy.

Still, there was that time when he was mortal . . . after I'd written him that way, thanks to that enchantment the gods temporarily put on my writing. Ares was, well, all too human then. And it's a good thing that both of us remembered who and what he really was . . .

No. You do not want to get involved in any way with someone who thrives on cruelty.

I know, it sounds all very daring and deliciously wicked. But when you come right down to it, strip away all that black leather—no, wrong turn of phrase there.

Let's try again. I've seen more battlefields than I would ever have chosen to see. And believe me, when you take away all the fake glamour, the black leather and the shining spears and all that, what you have left is one very unromantic fact:

The god of war may be dangerously handsome.

But war, my friends, is not.

I Scrub Your Back,
You Scrub Mine

Now, here's an issue that's really three lessons in one:

When a Warrior Princess has been out on the road for a long, *long* time, what's the first thing she wants when she finally reaches a town?

No, not *that!* Unless you are trying to attract a Centaur, the reek of sweaty horse just isn't going to do the trick. (Salmoneus once tried selling the Centaurs a fragrance he called Eau d'Equine, but that's a different story, and besides, they managed to get all those mares away from him before anyone got hurt.)

Back to that hot, sweaty warrior. What she wants first and foremost is a bath, a nice, hot bath with plenty of soap and no one pestering her to hurry up. Trust me on this one. Unless you have been out on the road for quite a while, particularly in the dry, dusty season, you have no idea just how heavenly a tub of hot water, lots of soap, and no pressing engagements can be!

Oh, and ideally, there should be room enough in that tub for two.

Why two?

Get your minds away from *that*, would you?

You want two because, quite simply, no wise Warrior Princess ever leaves her back unguarded! Besides, there are all those itchy spots between the shoulder blades that you just . . . can't . . . reach by yourself . . .

What about the lessons learned?

One, cleanliness is next to gods-liness, and a clean Warrior Princess gathers more friends.

Two, never leave your back unguarded.

And three, be fair! Don't hog all the soap!

"I love the smell of warrior sweat
in the morning."

Xena, "The Furies"

GOOD THINGS COME
IN SMALL PACKAGES

Why oh why do all the bards—all the *other* bards, that is—always insist on portraying heroes as tall? I mean, it's bad enough that we're still being confronted by the other nasty isms, like racism. Isn't "heightism" a little (sorry) bit ridiculous?

Actually, I'm thinking of one hero in particular: Iolaus. You must have heard of him. He's Hercules' friend, almost like a brother to him.

Which, I guess, is part of the problem. I mean, everyone's heard of Hercules. It's difficult not to notice someone like him: tall, golden, and half-god. And, well, let's face it, Iolaus, though he's just as nice-looking, *is* somewhat on the short side.

But what has height got to do with it? He's every bit as brave as Hercules, maybe even more so, since he doesn't have that half-divine blood to protect him! Iolaus is true and kind and—

And can you tell we almost . . . uh, well, I'm not really sure what might have happened. Let's just say we were drawn to each other, then realized it simply wasn't meant to be.

Don't believe that Iolaus is as heroic as Hercules? What about when all four of us, Xena and I, Hercules and Iolaus, set out on our epic quest to rescue Prometheus? Sure, Hercules was in danger, too—but it's really hard to kill or even seriously damage a half-god. It was Iolaus, all mortal and all brave, who was wounded so badly I was scared he'd die. That's when I tried to comfort him with the fable about people spending all their lives looking for the other halves of their souls.

Just then, I guess I thought, or maybe hoped, that Iolaus might be the other half of my soul.

But, hey, whatever else happened, or didn't happen, I learned one important lesson during that journey, when I wasn't sure if Iolaus was going to survive. Heroism knows no size.

That's right. Size really doesn't matter.

Except, of course, when we're talking about the size of a man's heart. And soul.

LEAVE *SOME*
STONES UNTURNED

Well, how was I supposed to know? I mean, what would you do if you came across three poor souls trapped in stone?

That those three poor souls happened not to be human beings but Titans, yes, I guess I should have been a little wary, but . . .

All right, I confess it. My curiosity, as well as my pity, and maybe a little bit of my pride—maybe a lot of my pride—got the better of me. Besides, the thought of reading that ancient scroll—I defy any bard, anyone with any sort of scholarly education, to resist that lure!

And let's be honest here: Who isn't going to enjoy a chance to be worshiped like a god? For . . . a short time, anyhow.

But still: How was I supposed to know that I'd wind up freeing not three very thankful Titans, but two reasonable and one very resentful one!

I mean, that's gratitude for you! Here I went and freed them, and all Hyperion—that was the hotheaded Titan—

all he could do was demand that I free hundreds more Titans. Why? So they could storm Mount Olympus, challenge the gods, and rule the whole world!

Now that really is going too far.

Everything that happened seemed to lead to something worse. Hyperion fought and killed a fellow Titan. And then he took out his anger and frustration on a village. It's a good thing Xena was there, because I know that I couldn't have stopped him alone. Hyperion would have destroyed that village and everyone in it if it hadn't been for her.

And I . . . well, I admit I made a few mistakes during the whole affair. More than a few. But you do have to take responsibility for your actions, like it or not.

What did I do? Well, let's just say that what gets transformed once can get transformed again. It wasn't easy, but I finally managed to chant a second spell.

And Hyperion, let's say, found it an absolutely . . . petrifying experience.

A FISH IN THE HAND
IS WORTH TWO IN THE
STREAM

Now, here's a question I hear a good deal—usually from those women who've never been out of sight of their own hearth fires:

"How can two women manage to survive out there in the wilderness?"

The answer, thank you very much, is that we can, and quite well, too. Xena's been on her own long enough to know what's safe to eat and what's best left alone, and she's taught me as well.

A few tips: Never try to eat any plant with a milky sap unless you plan on dying painfully; never touch any plant with leaves in bunches of three unless you plan to itch till you *want* to die; and never eat anything that starts talking to you. The gods sometimes play funny tricks.

Of course, it's not all sweetness and sunlight.

Sunlight, hah! Funny how it's always a bright, sunny

day when the bards sing about adventures. But, yes, if you travel in wilderness, sooner or later it's going to rain. Not the good, quick, crops-nourishing rain, but the steady, chilly, nasty stuff that gets into everything, and Argo pins her ears and tries to bite, and Xena has to keep checking to be sure her sword isn't getting rusty, and we both start losing our tempers over just about anything.

You manage. You grit your teeth and keep going and tell yourself that sooner or later you're either going to see an inn or, gods willing, sunshine.

And sure enough, the sun does come out again. Eventually. And if you are still speaking to your friend, no harm's done. Even if you *aren't* still speaking to your friend, you can at least start muttering apologies and know that sooner or later you or she is going to start laughing and forget the hard feelings.

As for fishing . . . it's true, I always *had* wanted to try that. You know what I mean. Reaching down and snatching a fish out of the water with nothing but your bare hands. And, yes, it can be done. You just have to move slowly, carefully, and . . .

Pounce!

And if you do it just right, you get that nice, wet, floppy fish onto the shore where you meant it to land and not hit your friend in the face with it or startle Argo or send the fish flying right back into the water again.

They don't sing about those mishaps in the bardic songs, either.

But eventually, as I say, the sun comes out, the rain dries

A Fish in the Hand Is Worth Two in the Stream

up, there's a fish roasting on the fire, you're sitting beside the best friend you've ever had, and you suddenly realize, hey, life's good.

And you wouldn't trade any of it for a safe, protected, really boring little hearth fire.

ANYTHING CAN BE A
WEAPON — ANYTHING!

W e've all heard that epic "Of arms and the man I sing." Here's the question, though: When you think *warrior,* what kinds of arms do you picture? A sword, maybe, or a spear or ax.

But that's only part of the story. One of the things I learned from Xena is, when defending yourself, be creative!

No, this doesn't mean that you should challenge the enemy to a contest about who can make the prettiest artwork out of paper flowers! But . . . what if you challenged him to a riddling contest? That would stop him from attacking you long enough for you to slip away while he was thinking things over. Or, if you're really good at riddles, you could trick him into surrendering when he can't solve them.

And that is one valuable weapon for you to use: your wits.

But suppose riddles and word tricks are the last things in your mind. Nothing wrong with that; not everyone's good at improvisational theater. You still have other weapons—namely, just about anything that comes to hand!

Don't believe me? How about a frying pan? I remember that one very well, because while Xena did defend us against several attackers using a pan as her weapon, she dented the thing—and curse it all, that was our only frying pan!

All right, never mind, that's in the past, and it was that sort of day anyhow. Now I can look back and say that Xena was right, saving our hides was more important than frying up a fish or two.

No frying pan? Not a problem!

Fish, I said, and there's a weapon. Don't believe me? Ever been smacked in the face by a flounder? Or sent a school of smelts flying in a makeshift catapult? Believe me, it's enough to bring a strong man to his knees.

Especially on a warm day when the fish have been out of the water a bit too long.

Ah, and there's one last weapon: you. Let's face it, human nature being what it is, if you step out of the water naked, you're going to have those of the other gender too startled to move, at least for a few precious moments.

Long enough for you to hit them with the frying pan or fish or, yes, the good old traditional sword.

So remember, next time someone attacks you, anything really can be used as a weapon!

"Fight now, talk later."
Xena, "Death Mask"

ONCE BITTEN, NOT SHY!

Remember when I talked about not becoming a "winer"? Well, there's worse. Far worse, because it all seems like such fun at first.

Our perilous friend Bacchus is to blame. Was? Is he dead? Really? I have my doubts about that. I mean, people are still getting drunk in his honor, aren't they?

Anyhow. Rather than get tangled up in the ways of the gods, I'll just say that if something looks like too much fun, it probably is.

I mean, that was one wild party the Bacchae were throwing: good music, weird dancing, the works. And I . . .

Well, you know how it goes. You think, the door's open, I'll just look inside. Then the music grabs you, and you think, I'll walk in just a little way, only a few steps, just to hear better, and then I'll leave.

Oh, right. The next thing that you know, you're in there dancing with everybody else and having a wild old time.

I admit it, that's what happened to me. What made it worse was that I knew the Bacchae were up to no good; I knew they were downright evil, with this really bad habit of tearing men apart. But the music was just so great, and the beat was just too tempting. After all, what harm could there be in just dancing?

A lot.

I don't remember all too much of what happened after that. Apparently, I got bitten and turned into a really ghastly Bacchae, fangs and yellow eyes and all, then flew off to join my fellow, uh, things to get a sip of Bacchus' blood. That would have turned me into a Bacchae permanently—

But of course Xena hadn't abandoned me. Together, we got rid of Bacchus (at least I *think* that we did, gods being what they are) and de-Bacchae-ed me.

A narrow escape all 'round. But a good lesson came out of that bad experience, and I'll sum it up for you in one sentence:

Don't follow the beat unless you trust the drummer!

You Don't Need a
Poetic License

I'm a bard. I like being one, and I like knowing I've got the talent to be one.

But becoming a bard doesn't mean I've also become some sort of mystical being: I'm still *me*, and I always was *me*, even when I felt I had something to prove.

I mean, much as I love Xena, there were times back then in my pre-bard days when I would rather not have been her sidekick. Not *only* her sidekick, rather, but her equal. In my own way, of course.

I guess it must be how Iolaus feels about Hercules: brotherly love, good friends to the death and all that, but it's still nice to know you have your own talents.

That's why, really, I decided to go to Athens, to that contest at the Athens City Academy of the Performing Bards. I didn't realize it at the time, but I think I was a little jealous of Xena, in bad need of finding out that I was more than just "the Warrior Princess's sidekick."

Which, ta-da, I learned. Not without some difficulties along the way, of course. It's not true that I cheated to get into that contest, only . . . bent the rules a little. And I certainly did nothing illegal to win! It was tough. Homer is good, he's really, really good.

Getting back to the contest: I hadn't really planned to tell the story of my adventures with Xena; the judges, I thought, were looking for something less, well, realistic. But when it came time to perform, something happened inside. Suddenly I just couldn't give some standard poem or epic saga. I spoke from the heart.

And that was when I realized something: I hadn't really needed to win that contest. Oh, it was fun, don't get me wrong! You're not getting that parchment back from me!

But I didn't need the formal recognition. I was a bard. I'd always been one. And that was my own special gift.

That's right: I really didn't need to take that poetic license.

SEA? SAW!

Don't get me wrong. I have nothing personal against Poseidon—or, hear me, gods, against any of you! I know that the sea is full of all sorts of wonders. I know that we need it and that many people's lives and livelihoods depend on it. In fact, I think that the sea is quite beautiful to look at.

From a distance.

A safe distance.

Every time I actually get on the sea, no matter in whose boat or ship, something seems to go wrong. I've already mentioned how miserably seasick I was aboard Ulysses' ship. They tell you with what I think is misplaced cheerfulness that no one ever died of seasickness. That's only because when you're seasick, you're too weak to kill them.

But, difficult as it may be to believe while you are seasick, worse perils can befall you. Remember that Poseidon was really angry at Ulysses—and that his anger extended to anyone on Ulysses' ship. Including me. I've had the less than fun experience of being thrown overboard, only to be rescued by Cecrops.

Right. That Cecrops. The fellow who'd been cursed by

Poseidon. Or rather, the *other* fellow who'd been cursed by Poseidon, this one for choosing Athena over the god of the sea as his city's patron. That left poor Cecrops trapped, doomed to forever sail the seas. And, guess what? Anyone who set foot on his ship was stuck there, too.

Only, thank the gods for Xena, it didn't end up that way. Yes, she got aboard, and yes, Cecrops, with her help, did break the curse. He's wandering blessedly dry land right now, doing good deeds as he goes.

And me? You can already guess what happened. Sure enough, I got miserably seasick all over again while I was trapped on Cecrops' ship. Xena came to the rescue with a pressure point that does seem to stop the nausea.

But that doesn't mean something else won't go wrong the next time I step aboard a ship.

Though, come to think of it, maybe I can risk sailing again. After all, I've eaten raw squid.

Surely there can't be anything worse than that!

The God of War Is Not an Equal Opportunity Employer

I've mentioned Ares before, of course. How could I not, considering what Xena is—and what she used to be. And of course it doesn't help that the god of war is always keeping an eye on her, hoping that the Warrior Princess will slide back to her old, dark ways.

Keeping an eye on her? Hah! He downright tries to push! Ares is determined to win Xena back to the dark side in any way possible.

But then, what do you expect from him? He's only acting according to his nature. Like a snake. A handsome one, granted, but quite able to bite you where and when you least expect it.

Such as when . . . well, it's a complex tale. Let's just say that Xena and I were about to rescue some women from a warlord when an older man got in the way. We did rescue the women—but then the older man claimed to be Xena's father.

Right. I suspected a snake almost from the start.

Or at least I think I did. Like everyone else, I have flawless hindsight!

Anyhow, when we took the rescued women to their village, one thing led to another. Xena fought and defeated the warlord, then returned to find that the villagers had killed her father.

Again, right. You can guess what happened. Xena, raging, nearly reverted to her bad old ways there and then. And I, well, I did what I had to do, arguing with her and finally, yes, hitting her, hard.

And that, of course, was when good old Gorgeous Black Leather Snake, Ares himself, miraculously changed from old man to himself and came back from the "dead," taunting Xena.

Scary thought: *Is* he really her father? Or was that just another of Ares' lies?

Well. Whatever the truth, I'm always there for Xena. And, gods willing, I always will be.

Whether Ares likes it or not.

"Her courage would change the world...."

Xena, Gabrielle, and Joxer celebrate a heroic job well done... and done... and done... "Been There, Done That."

Xena and Gabby share a moment atop Argo—before being driven apart in "The Debt."

The Warrior Princess and her favorite bard consider their options in "The Dirty Half Dozen."

Gabrielle speaks softly and swings a big stick in "The Dirty Half Dozen."

Can even the Warrior Princess stand against warriors clad in the invulnerable metal of Hephæstus?

Another day, another challenge in "The Furies."

Driven mad in "The Furies,"
the Warrior Princess
threatens her best friend.

Xena is on guard against
banshees in "Gabrielle's Hope."

Xena stalks the private
chambers of Cleopatra
in search of the
"King of Assassins."

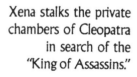

A vengeful Warrior Princess takes aim against Callisto in "Maternal Instincts."

After a long day fishing, Xena finds a creative use for eel in "The Quill Is Mightier. . . ."

In the Temple of Dahak, Xena faces the demonic strength of "The Deliverer."

Britannia holds hidden perils for Xena in "The Deliverer."

e Warrior Princess
ngs into action in
omedy of Eros."

Danger lurks in the forest
of the Bacchae in "Girls
Just Wanna Have Fun."

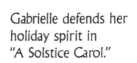

Gabrielle defends her
holiday spirit in
"A Solstice Carol."

Ares, god of war, will stop at nothing to reclaim his Warrior Princess.

Horsing Around

I t occurs to me that I haven't been giving Argo her due. After all, she puts up with me, hasn't bitten me more than that once (accidentally, I think), and stepped on me only twice (I think that was an accident, too, though I'd swear she was watching me all the while the second time around).

But then, Argo isn't exactly a dumb animal. I'm not saying she holds long conversations with either Xena or me, but she certainly does comment in horsey fashion, whinnying or snorting as though she knows perfectly well what's going on.

Maybe she does! There was that time when Xena was about to be torn apart by "wild horses," one of which, thanks to me, was Argo. I swear that Argo somehow told that other horse not to move!

Could be.

Anyhow, a few rules of horsewomanship might fit in here, I think. Such as: You groom a horse firmly, not gently. Gently tickles. You let a horse graze, yes, but you get that horse good, nourishing grain whenever you can; grass just doesn't have enough food value. Oh, and a horse isn't a magic machine: you don't just leap on and ride off at whirlwind speed, nor do you keep riding at a full gallop all day.

Of course, if the horse happens to be Pegasus, all bets, as the saying goes, are off. But then, Pegasus doesn't have to worry about galloping. Not on the ground, anyhow.

Back to Argo. There are certain spots she really likes scratched, and Xena obliges. It's really nice to see the two of them together, Argo leaning her head against the Warrior Princess, while said Princess scratches the mare behind her ears. Those two do understand each other, no doubt about it!

Yes, Argo's a smart, sweet, clever horse. She's all the things you want to see in a horse, in fact.

And now, Argo, assuming you really do understand more than you're letting on, will you kindly get your foot off the edge of my cloak so I can move?

Thank you.

WHEELING AND DEALING

Funny how often chariot races seem to turn up in my adventures with Xena. Or maybe it's not so funny at that, because they can be wonderful ways to settle an issue. Instead of a duel to the death, you can substitute a chariot race in which no one gets hurt.

Ah, no, make that a chariot race in which no one is supposed to get hurt! Things don't always happen the way you want. Or expect.

Look at what happened when we came across that vicious warlord Sphaerus, and his son, Cycnus. Sphaerus was all set to continue on his conquering; Xena was all for stopping him. But things didn't work out the way I'd thought they would.

For one thing, Xena was wounded and treated by Darius, a gentle man who showed her that a life of peace isn't such a bad thing. I think it was the first time that my friend realized that *peaceful* doesn't necessarily mean "weak," and I also think she was genuinely tempted to settle down with him.

But his life wasn't meant to be hers.

As for me, I learned from Cycnus not to judge people by

first appearances, because it turned out that Cycnus wasn't like his bloodthirsty father at all; he hated the horrible things Sphaerus was doing. In fact, Cycnus was, underneath it all, very nice, indeed, and given a little more time, he and I just might have . . .

Never mind what-might-have-beens. Back to the chariots, and the chariot race between Xena and Cycnus. The one that Xena won. Of course, she did have to kill Sphaerus after it, but that's another matter. It was the chariot race that really brought about a final peaceful resolution.

Of course, a settlement can only be reached if both sides want one. In bardic honesty, I have to mention Callisto. She and Xena held a chariot race, too, but that one hardly ended peacefully. Yes, Callisto died when she fell into that quicksand, and that was definitely the finish of that race! I admit that it's a nasty way for anyone to go, but of course, that . . . woman . . . is just too evil to politely stay dead.

But once again, that's another story.

"It ain't over till it's over."

Xena, "Return of Callisto"

IF YOU THINK THAT YOU'RE DREAMING, PINCH YOURSELF. IF THAT DOESN'T WORK, PINCH SOMEONE ELSE

Morpheus, they say, is related to Hades, god of the underworld. That may be, although Hades seems to be a pretty nice guy despite his job, someone who is genuinely devoted to his wife, Persephone. But I, for one, am not about to go to either of their realms, Morpheus or Hades, to ask them about their families.

I've already been to the so-called Land of Dreams, or at least to Morpheus' castle, and believe me, "nightmare" is more like it.

Though it was Xena who suffered the true nightmare.

Let's see if I can get this straight: I was caught by the priests of Morpheus, who decided, "Isn't this jolly, she hasn't killed anyone, so she'll make a *perfect* sacrifice," i.e., just the right bride for Morpheus, who apparently needs a new one every solstice.

You don't want to know what happens to the old ones. Yes, and then, to make the perfect sacrifice even more perfect, I was supposed to be goaded into killing someone. Not a chance. I hadn't realized till that moment just how much I'd learned about fighting and *not* killing from Xena.

Who, meanwhile, was undergoing her own eerie dream quest to find me, and battling the demons of her own soul. From what she's told me, she had to fight herself, metaphysically speaking, only to realize that the good or evil half of her was only part of the whole.

So there we have it: two lessons learned from that weird adventure.

One, you don't have to kill someone to win the battle.

And two, like it or not, we're all stuck with the dark side as well as the light side as part of who and what we are.

It's up to each and every one of us to decide which side to choose.

Beauty May Be in the Eye of the Beholder, but What If He's Nearsighted?

Oone of the questions I seem to hear the most from other women is "How do you manage to keep that fresh, girlish glow while on the road?"

I could just answer, smiling sweetly and blinking innocently, "Sunshine, fresh air, and clean living."

I could. But . . .

Sunshine is all well and good, ladies, but I hope that you all know too much of it isn't really healthy. Besides, that pretty tan today gives you skin like old leather tomorrow. Well-tanned old leather.

What you don't hear the bards singing about is that the wise Warrior Princess keeps a vial of lotion in her pack for her face and hands. No, this isn't merely vanity. It's a lot easier to grip a sword or staff properly if your hands are supple.

Now, as for that nice, fresh air: Yes, it's good for you. If it is fresh, but not too raw. Wind-roughened skin isn't so attractive, and when you're in the middle of wilderness, chapped skin can be downright dangerous, since it's not exactly dirt-free and clean in that wilderness. If the wind's too raw, get out that shawl or scarf and wrap it about your face.

Leaving your eyes free, of course; I watched a clumsy dancer once get her veil so tangled over her face that she couldn't see anything and fell right into the king's lap. Fortunately, she was pretty, so I don't think he minded too much!

Anyhow, on to clean living! Ah, the wholesome life in forest and field.

Ah, the mosquitoes!

Ah, the rain and mud!

Particularly the mud.

Mud baths may be fashionable and good for your skin—but they're no fun if the pigs have been in there first and you fall in afterward.

That's when you discover the joys of bathing in the fresh, clean, freeze-your-toes-off river because you can't wait to get that smell off you.

Yes, ladies, there you have it: sunshine, fresh air, and clean living will do you in every time!

NO BOYS ALLOWED!

I'll say right from the start that I never deliberately set out to become an Amazon, let alone an Amazon princess and the Amazon queen. These things just . . . well, they sort of just happen.

However, I learned a good deal in the brief time I was with the Amazons. Oh, did I ever! And that started with the realization that I was willing to protect someone I didn't even really know, Terreis, the Amazon queen's wounded sister.

That's when I learned something else: in Amazon society, something called Right of Cast can be transferable. And since poor Terreis was too badly injured to survive, that left me suddenly not little Gabrielle, the girl from a small village, but royal Gabrielle, Amazon princess.

Sounds pretty nice, doesn't it? It meant living as an Amazon for a time, which was fascinating. The Amazons have an incredibly intricate society, most of which I'm not at liberty to discuss. But I will say that the dancing and chants are a lot of fun, even if the masks everyone wears for rituals are hot and uncomfortable. Not that you're supposed to notice such "unworthy" matters!

But of course there's much more to being Amazon princess than just singing and dancing. There's fighting. And . . . there's killing. It wasn't until another Amazon, Ephiny, showed me how I could use a staff to kill a Centaur that the truth suddenly struck home. This was no game. People could die.

I think I got a giant dose of "grow up fast" just then, particularly since as Amazon princess I was supposed to kill a Centaur who'd been accused of Terreis' death. Wrongly accused, as it happened. And fortunately, Xena and I were able to prove his innocence before he could be slain or the Amazons and Centaurs could go to war.

But I didn't forget the lessons learned.

Particularly the most serious: Weapons are not toys. Use them, and people get hurt.

Misuse them, and the wrong people just may get killed.

"The moment you pick up a sword,
you become a target."

Xena, "Dreamworker"

A Woman's Gotta Do What a Woman's Gotta Do

What I mean by that is choices. We all face them, we all make them.

But sometimes you need to make the right choice for the right reason, for the Greater Good. No matter how difficult that might be.

Of course, the biggest choice I ever made was to completely change my life by leaving home and joining Xena on her adventures. Now, there's a choice I never regret! Almost never, anyhow, since there are times during those cold, muddy, rainy days . . . Well, we all have *those* days no matter what life we're leading.

Another major choice I made would have changed my life again. Yes, I became an Amazon princess, but mainly because at the time I hadn't a clue as to what choices that involved. Later, I could have become Amazon queen— but now I did know what that entailed, and I chose not to accept the title. Why? Two reasons, only one of them selfish. No, I didn't really want to give up my life with Xena—but I also knew that I'd make a terrible queen and turned down the title for the sake of the Amazons.

Choices. When I'd left home, remember that I'd also left my fiancé, Perdicas. I had never really expected to see him again—but I did, much later. We'd both changed by then, both done a good amount of growing up, and . . . no choice about that, I fell in love with him. And I chose to marry him. Had he lived . . . well, if he had, I would be a very different woman now, a settled wife and, maybe, mother . . .

Choices, again. When the vengeful and pretty much insane Amazon Velasca ate some ambrosia, making her more or less a goddess, wreaking horror, Xena and I knew that only another immortal could stop her: Callisto, who had eaten from the Tree of Life. I had to make maybe the most painful choice of my life just then. I could either work with Callisto,—the murderer of my poor Perdicas— or I could try to kill her, this time for good.

What choice did I make? Well, let's just say that it wasn't easy, but at least now the world is safe from immortal, psychotic Amazons.

"Hard times make hard people."

Xena, "Hercules: The Warrior Princess"

WINSOME AND LOSE SOME

Aphrodite doesn't play fair.

She doesn't have to. She's a goddess. But she does seem to have a weird sense of humor even for a goddess.

I mean, look at what happened when her son, Cupid, had the nerve to fall in love with a mortal woman—yes, and then when their son stole Papa's enchanted arrows . . .

Well, that was really a bizarre time, everybody in love with everybody else, whether it made sense or not. I mean, I admit it, I seem to have bad luck with men. But to fall for *Joxer?*

Of course, some of my other choices have been less than perfect. My lifestyle has a good deal to do with it. There aren't all that many men who are willing to put up with a girlfriend who's never going to be there long enough to settle down.

Though I was willing to settle down . . . with Perdicas . . .

Never mind. What happened, happened, and not even the gods can change the past.

Now, as for Iolaus and me . . . well, that never quite got

beyond the mutual lust stage. Besides, he had his life, I had mine, and no hard feelings.

Besides, I always did have a soft spot for the poetic type. Like Talus. I remember the two of us healing someone together, and thinking how nice it was to see a man who could care about another. He also was quite a good storyteller, and I think that's what drew us together, the stories we knew in common. But . . . well . . . our affair was doomed from the start, because Talus was quite literally living on borrowed time. And much as I hated, and still hate, the idea, he *had* to die.

But, back to Aphrodite before I start singing sad songs. I don't know this for sure, of course, but maybe, just maybe, she's become more sympathetic to mortals. After all, there was that time when she, too, was mortal, and finding out that life is not a bowl of ambrosia for us. Maybe she'll think just a tiny bit longer before sending out Cupid and his arrows.

After all, thanks to those arrows, love can quite literally be a pain!

THE CASE OF THE
COPIED PRINCESS

Now, see if you can spot the lesson I learned in the following adventure.

Adventure? Misadventure, really. And all thanks to our old merchant friend, Salmoneus. You know him, always out to corner the market on something new and exciting—and always having the market corner him instead.

This time, he had taken on a new identity as Lord Seltzer and was selling fizzy water. That would have worked nicely, since folks seemed to like it, but Salmoneus never does seem to know when to leave well enough alone. He was also selling something known as talgamite, weird stuff that could be made into pretty swords but which unfortunately melted in the rain.

Not surprisingly, those suddenly melting weapons infuriated the lord he'd sold them to, Talmadeus, a man with a really terrible temper.

You see the picture being painted here, don't you? It was Xena and me to the rescue!

Unfortunately, things didn't work quite that way. Xena

was felled by a drugged dart (blown by our old nonfriend Callisto, though we didn't know that at the time). And so, since *someone* had to be Xena . . .

Ta-da, enter Gabrielle, Warrior Princess. More or less. My one big moment of playacting, and I . . . well, to be honest, I pretty much fouled it up.

In short, I made a terrible Xena, but once I was captured, I did a nice job as me and escaped.

Much confusion followed, including a stellar turn on-stage by Argo, who, as I mentioned earlier, refused to allow another horse to tear Xena limb from limb. In the end, the gods be praised, Xena recovered, and Talmadeus learned the error of his way.

That was his lesson.

Mine?

Surely it's obvious after that disastrous turn "onstage" as Xena. I make a fine bard but a terrible impersonator. The lesson is:

Be yourself. Unless, of course, you really *can* do a better job as someone else!

"My name is Xena.
I'm a problem-solver."

Xena, "The Black Wolf"

SEEING DOUBLE ... NO, MAKE THAT TRIPLE ... NO, QUADRUPLE

L et me state right here and now that there is only one Gabrielle, one me.

At least, as far as I know.

In Xena's case, of course, all bets are off. Someone in her ancestry seems to have been married more times than good old Polygamous! Or else, the gods liked the pattern of her so much they decided to repeat it. Again. And again. And again!

I think we've seen all the variants.

Maybe.

Let's see now . . .

The first one I met was, of course, *the* Xena. There's no one like her!

But then . . . Xena had been off on a brief journey, and of course when I saw—well, for a few confused moments, I thought I was seeing her returned. But then, uh, I realized that this was one strange Xena! No fighting skills, no courage, no knowledge of the real world, and a lot of weepiness.

Of course it turned out to be Princess Diana, and Xena and I got her safely married to her true love, Prince Philemon.

Then there was the second not-Xena, Meg, the . . . well, let's call her a barmaid. Nice, cheerful gal with rather, ah, loose standards. And very much not a Warrior Princess!

All right. One Xena, one princess (not warrior), one barmaid (definitely not princess). That, I thought, was the end of that.

Wrong!

Now I was faced with a shy and retiring . . . Xena? No, of course not. This not-Xena was, of all things, a vestal virgin!

And now we had . . . Xena (Warrior Princess), Diana (royal princess), Meg (no princess), and one pure and wholesome vestal virgin. Mix well, and you can understand why for a time no one knew which Xena was which!

Oh, I hope that four of them is the core of them, that there really are no more of them!

OF HEALING AND REVEALING

I don't want to give the impression that all I learned from Xena—aside, of course, from major things such as friendship and wilderness survival—was warfare. Far from it! Xena is quite an accomplished healer, to the point that she downright amazes me.

She won't tell me where she learned what she knows, either. Which, now that I think about it, extends from medical skills to an awful lot about her.

Oh, well, her past history is her business, not mine!

Though I do wonder . . .

But I'm digressing. Xena is teaching me a good deal about healing, too. I've learned a fair amount about which herbs are good for what ailments, such as comfrey for bruises or arnica for sprains. You have to watch out, though, because a lot of herbs can be toxic in too large a dosage. The thought of accidentally poisoning someone I'm trying to help is frightening enough to keep me very, very careful!

Oh, but there are nice side uses for herbs, too! Ladies, you'll probably be more interested in this than will be the gentlemen. Not that there's anything wrong in a gentleman wanting to do something about the color of his hair. There. The secret's out. No, I do *not* dye my hair; I really am a blonde. But when you're out of doors so much, the sun bleaches your hair to, well, straw. And so I do use a chamomile rinse, which brightens the color. And that's why sometimes my hair does look more reddish than others.

No, Xena does *not* color her hair. Not that you really needed to know. But if she did, well, chestnut makes a nice dye for dark hair.

And of course, there's the old trick most country women learn: berry stain for the lips and cheeks. Not that I use that. Not often, anyhow. Just when we're going into town and I want to look my best.

There you have it: beauty secrets of the wandering bard.

HIDE-AND-SEEK

Everyone has heard tales of marvelous buried treasures and bloodstained treasure maps. Sounds wonderfully exciting, doesn't it? Almost romantic.

Well, I've been there, and I've done that, and there wasn't all that much romantic about it.

Of course, there *was* Petracles . . . but he wasn't interested in me, not really.

Besides, there was nothing at all romantic about what we were hunting. Danger, yes, beyond all mortal perils (which is often what Xena and I seem to be hunting), but no romance.

It's not the first time that Xena and I have gone off on a quest. However, we don't usually go with a couple of not exactly trustworthy men, one of whom—yes, Petracles—turned out to be none other than Xena's ex-fiancé.

Now, there was a really interesting complication, and one I really didn't want.

Never mind that. The point of this particular treasure hunt wasn't the gems or gold you'd expect to be seeking.

It was ambrosia.

That's right. The food of the gods. Any mortal who

tastes ambrosia gains instant immortality. And Xena, of course, wasn't about to let something so dangerous and powerful fall into the wrong hands.

She wasn't about to let me fall into the wrong hands, either. Along the way, Petracles started to flirt with me. Really flirt. I don't know if Xena was jealous, or just watching out for me, and I don't really want to know, either. It was bad enough hearing her tell how when she was much younger he had wooed her, then abandoned her.

But you can't always know someone, really know them. Our treasure hunt ended on a note of tragic heroism. The other treasure seeker in our little group, Thersites, had no redeeming social values. He tried to use me as a hostage to get him the ambrosia, and Petracles rescued me—only to be mortally wounded in the process. Xena, of course, returned that perilous ambrosia to the gods, where it belonged.

Then . . . oh, it was like something out of a bard's tale. As he died in her arms, Petracles returned to Xena the wedding bracelet she'd given him so many years ago.

He'd loved her all along, I guess.

As I say, you really can't always judge a man by the company he keeps.

WAR AND MORE OR LESS PEACE

Lt took me a long time to accept, even with all the evidence before me, just how much violence there is in our world. I know Xena would say I was being naive.

But I also know that there's a side to her that's as disgusted by war as I am. And I don't mean just Xena's valiant efforts to stay on the side of Light. I mean . . .

Well, think about those healer skills of hers. Yes, a military doctor has to be good at patching up warriors so they can go back into battle. But . . .

I remember when Xena and I were trapped in the middle of a war in Thessaly. We'd set up a makeshift hospital in one of the temples, and Xena—well, she was doing more than just patching people up. She was really getting into the saving of lives. I saw her do some pretty remarkable things, utterly ignoring the traditional stuff that priest, what's-his-name, Galen, was insisting that she use: stuff that would have killed as many as it saved.

And . . . I have a personal interest in Xena's medical skills, because she saved my life. I got wounded in that stupid war, went into shock, and . . . well . . . apparently, I died. That might be, because I have a vague memory of being somehow outside my body, not knowing if I should stay or go, and dimly hearing Xena shouting at me, "Don't you leave me!"

I guess that it happened. The whole thing is a little hazy by now.

Anyhow, Xena brought me back to life, that much I do know.

And then she did something else that was above and beyond what a warrior turned doctor out of need would do. I don't know because she won't talk about it, but I think somewhere in that hospital, surrounded by all the desperately hurt, Xena got so disgusted by war that she determined to at least stop this one.

And she did it. Xena forced General Marmax to see, truly see, what was happening, all the useless suffering and death—and she got him to make peace with his enemy.

Amazing, isn't it?

Beauty May Be Only Skin-Deep, but Who Wants to Walk Around in Her Bare Bones?

Now, before you start complaining, that's meant as a sarcastic title. Honest. People have some really weird, really set ideas of who's beautiful and who isn't, and an awful lot of folks still think that a woman's only importance is as an art object. You know, someone who gets put up on that pedestal like a statue? Unless you're into being turned to stone, that's a really stupid place for a human being to be.

Anyhow, I was lucky enough to be present when a certain archaic ritual got turned upside down.

Of course, there was a decent concept behind this particular beauty pageant, namely to celebrate a year of holding together a truce of peace. But since our old friend Salmoneus was behind the pageant, I have to wonder just how pure the concept was.

No, I don't. I *know*. Salmoneus was out to make some dinars.

Now, of course, whenever Salmoneus is involved, things don't run precisely according to plan. And in this case, someone was out to sabotage the pageant and in the process break the truce. So there we were, Xena and I, in disguise: Miss Amphipolis—Xena—and her agent, me. That's when I saw up close what an archaic ritual this was. I mean, it's one thing to put mares on display, check out their conformation, their breeding potential. But when you do the same thing to human beings, female or male, why, you're taking away all their dignity and intelligence.

Well, we managed to strike a blow for human freedom. I . . . guess. Oh, Xena caught the would-be saboteur easily enough. But she also found out something else: one of the contestants was, well, very special.

Very . . . different, shall we say?

And when this special contestant, Miss Artyphis, won, it was a moment to be cherished, indeed. For Miss Artyphis isn't a woman at all!

Now, some people say that when s/he kissed Xena, I got jealous. Of course I did—in a very human way. Do you blame me? Any woman would be jealous of someone who, regardless of gender, looked prettier than anyone else in the room!

STRANGERS IN THE NIGHT

Of course, we all know that, to humans, anyway, the night seems more mysterious, even more perilous, than the day.

It is. Both. But not always in the way you might think. I mean, the occasional bandit does try to blunder his way to your camp in the dark, and there are certain Things that prefer to wander about in the night, but both of them aren't a match for a Warrior Princess, a bard with a ready staff, and a horse who knows how to kick a bandit or Thing where it will do the most good.

So. The perils are more like this:

It's the middle of the night, and—

A noise! A . . . loud, steady, disturbing noise.

No, Xena doesn't snore. Argo, however, does.

Ah. She's stopped, waking up, as horses do, to graze a midnight snack. I can get back to sleep.

Can I?

We've camped near a stream: nice, peaceful sound of babbling brook. Just when I am drifting back off to sleep . . .

Splat!

I wake with a start. But—no monster. Nothing but a fish slapping the water with its tail.

Back to sleep . . .

Crack!

Bandits! No. A dead branch hit the ground, that's all.

Now I'm wide-awake, lying there wrapped up in my cloak. I should have remembered to dig a hole in the ground for my hipbone, but I didn't, so every time I try to roll over, ow. And there are pebbles that somehow have grown to boulders there under my right shoulder blade.

Ah, and the children of the night, listen to them—they never shut up! The little children, that is, the crawling, creeping, chattering ones. The crickets, in particular, one of which is perched nearby, yelling in my ear. I make a blind swat, miss, lose my cloak, sit up, swearing silently, find the cloak, wipe away the pebbles, and dig at least a dent in the ground for my hipbone.

During all this, Xena, of course, is sleeping like the proverbial innocent babe.

I lie back down, wrap myself in the cloak, resolutely shut my eyes, and . . . drift peacefully . . . off to sleep . . .

Only, of course, by now it's no longer night. And as the cursed birds start shouting overhead, I groan and rise to greet the new day.

EVERYBODY NEEDS SOME BODY SOMETIMES

I t has been pointed out by quite a few people who follow the stories of our adventures that those adventures can sometimes be, well, a little bit on the weird side.

Oh, I don't know about that, and, yes, I'm saying that sarcastically. What else can you expect *but* weirdness when gods and supposedly deceased but ever-returning psychotic warrior women get involved?

I'd heard about out-of-body experiences, you see, but I'd never expected to witness an into-body one. Or rather, an into-the-wrong-body experience.

Blame Ares. Of course blame Ares! First he looked up Callisto, who was already dead and in the underworld, then managed to trap Xena's spirit down there with Callisto. Me, I woke up to find what I thought was Xena acting really strangely—then realized that what I was facing was Callisto in a stolen guise. A Callisto determined to use Xena's body to help her gain power as a warlord.

Wonderful.

But it got stranger. Remember that I've said that Hades

really isn't such a bad sort. Well, he agreed with Xena that Ares was tampering in his domain, so he gave us at least a little help. When Xena confronted Callisto on the level of the dreamscape, Xena won—and woke up in Callisto's body. More problems for her, more trauma for me. And we won't even talk about Argo's reaction to someone who acted like Xena, but looked and smelled like Callisto—a Callisto who had tried to kill her!

All right, now, bear with me. We had Xena in Callisto's body, Callisto in Xena's body, and me trying desperately to figure out the truth.

Think that's complicated? Wait. Callisto wasn't the only escapee from the underworld. The late-but-determined not-to-stay-that-way King Sisyphus, who had been a tricky sort in life, in death stole Ares' sword, robbing him of power, and set up a contest: he who killeth the monster becometh god of war, or words to that effect.

Guess who won? Right. Xena in Callisto's body. And, yes, once the Ares' sword was returned to him, he had no choice but to make the body switch: Xena was now home where she belonged.

Now, I ask you, what's so weird about all that?

LOVE CAN BE A REAL PAIN

I mean, think about it: those arrows, that sudden sharp stab of longing—and not always for the logical person, either.

And it's all Aphrodite's fault. Not that she's a dark god like Ares. But she is a bit of a . . . well, let's just say that she's not the goddess of learning, after all!

Need some examples? Look at what happened when Aphrodite had set her mind against a political marriage that was also a love match. Why was she against it? Because the union of the two kingdoms might cause the downfall of some of her temples.

I mean, yes, that might be insulting to a goddess, but it's not as though she hasn't got plenty of other temples!

Getting back to Aphrodite, what did she do but cast a spell on poor, defenseless Joxer! Ring a bell, and he became the bravest, most romantic of warriors that ever came between lovers. Ring it again, and back to plain old foolish Joxer. He almost got killed thanks to Aphrodite's little ploy, and when I rang the bell to get Joxer back to the hero who could fight his way free, *I* almost got caught in his spell. Scary.

Scarier yet was when Cupid's son—Aphrodite's grandson, though I wouldn't want to be the mortal who called her Grandma—started shooting his father's arrows at anyone and everyone. Xena got hit and fell for the warlord Draco. He got hit and fell for me. I got hit and fell for, dare I say it, Joxer. Even Joxer thought that one was a little weird! I even sang a tribute for him, that never-ending "Joxer the Mighty," which has such deathless lines as, "Gabby as his sidekick / Fighting with her little stick." What do you want? I was under the influence of love.

So there we all were, running after each other. I don't know how it would all have ended, since Xena was, at the same time, trying to rescue some Hestial vestals from slavers. But fortunately, Xena was able to get Cupid to take parental responsibility and set everything right.

Almost. Draco is still, as far as I know, in love with me and determined to do only good deeds so that he can be worthy of me. And Joxer . . . well, Cupid's arrows or no, Joxer has always been in love with me.

Thank you so-o-o much, Aphrodite!

IF YOU HAVE A LION'S HEART, YOU'D BETTER BE A LIONESS

Let's discuss the meaning of a word that's bandied about all too easily: *courage.*

Now, there is a word that means a lot of different things to different people.

Take Joxer, for example. An unlikely sort of hero, isn't he? But why does he do the things he does, wandering about the countryside trying his best to play a hero's role no matter how many times he gets knocked down? Stupidity? Well, yes. But it also takes a genuine type of courage to hold on to your dream, to keep believing in yourself even when all the rest of the world is laughing at you.

And what about Xena? Not a fair example, you say. She's too well trained as a warrior, so she knows what she can do.

Right. But since she's seen more of battle than many warriors, Xena also has a clearer idea of what could happen to her. In her place, I think I might just freeze up in the middle of a battle and would probably get myself killed.

And let's not forget what Xena once was: a warlord very much on the side of the bad guys. The Darkness, as I'm sure everyone's learned at one time or another, is very, *very* seductive, and we're not just talking about Ares in that sexy black leather, either. Xena has to wage a constant battle with herself, and that's the toughest foe of all, fighting to keep from sliding back into the evil old ways. That definitely takes courage!

And what about me? Well, I never thought of myself as particularly brave. When I set out after Xena, as I've said, I was scared silly. And for a long time after that, I continued to believe that courage was something only warriors possessed.

Then I went home. And saw my village imperiled by a warlord. I didn't consciously set out to be brave. I didn't even worry about what might happen to me because, quite frankly, when you have friends and family at stake, you stop thinking only of yourself.

That's when it hit me. True courage isn't about warlords and battlefields. It can be seen all around us. Think of the mother in childbirth, or the father in his field fighting the elements day after day so that the crops will grow and his family will be fed.

True courage isn't about glamour or fame. It comes when you aren't worrying about bravery.

True courage is simply this: come what may, doing what has to be done.

KEEPING YOUR MIND WHEN
YOUR FRIEND IS LOSING HERS

You know how it is when you have a friend or family member who's always as steady as that proverbial rock. Then, when something happens, when they suddenly prove that you can no longer . . . forgive me . . . take them for granite, well, it's as shocking as though the world had suddenly turned to sand.

So it was for me when Xena, good, dependable, brave Xena, began all at once acting . . . silly. Increasingly, dangerously silly. Like dropping her sword in the middle of a fight, or jumping on Argo backward.

At first, I thought it was some weird sort of test of my abilities. You know, see what the girl can do under stress. Unfortunately, it wasn't a test, and the stress only increased, because Xena quickly proved she'd gone utterly, perilously, hallucinate-enemies-and-nearly-stab-your-friend insane.

I followed Xena, of course; you don't let your dearest friend go off like that alone. And that's when the whole thing started to make sense. Cyrene, Xena's mother, confessed to me that when her daughter was small, Xena was nearly sacrificed to Ares—by Cyrene's husband. And Cyrene, to save her daughter, had killed him. Ares. Right. The pattern was starting to make sense. The Furies, as you probably know, punish folks for failing to fulfill vital obligations, such as avenging a father's death. Even if Xena had never known that her mother had killed him. Who else but Ares to remind the Furies of this little situation?

The hero Orestes had gotten into a similar bind, because he'd had to kill his mother, who'd murdered her husband, the king. So off I went to Orestes—only to find, to my horror, that poor man still utterly mad.

Oh, yes, and meanwhile, while I was wondering what to do next, I was also wondering what Xena, armed and dangerous, was going to do to her mother. I hurried back—and sure enough, there he was, tall, dark, and vicious: Ares.

But guess what? The man Cyrene had killed was not Xena's father after all. Could the sire be . . . Ares? Nasty thought, isn't it? But at least this meant that Xena, who promptly fought Ares and won, was innocent of any lack of daughterly obligation. The Furies promptly returned her sanity, Ares left, still denying he was Xena's father, and I . . . well, I tiptoed away from the scene of mother and daughter comforting each other over what Cyrene had been forced to do.

There are, when you come right down to it, worse things than madness.

JOXERCISING

I've already mentioned the strange triplicate editions of Xena, namely Diana, Meg, and our sweet little vestal virgin. So far as I know, there are no doubles or triples of me wandering around—those . . . underclad dancing images of me that Joxer accidentally and, thank the gods, temporarily created don't count, since they never were real.

But Joxer, too, seems to have suffered a duplication, in the form of an identical twin brother, Jett.

The, dare I say it, Evil Twin.

Which might explain what went wrong with Joxer: he got all the nice but, well, dumb attributes, leaving "clever but nasty" for Jett.

And, of course, Joxer was promptly blamed for Jett's crimes. Which meant that even Autolycus, King of Thieves, who is a separate story in himself, was after Joxer until I showed him that this nice but clumsy fellow couldn't possibly be a cold-blooded killer.

But this situation had to be resolved before Joxer got killed in Jett's place. Particularly since Jett had been hired to assassinate none other than Cleopatra. Off the three of us went to the castle in which Cleopatra was staying.

Things got complicated about then, what with everyone thinking Joxer was Jett (at least briefly) and us getting arrested, me freeing myself and taking on the guise of an Egyptian slave girl so I could get close to Cleopatra—only to wind up back in prison.

Well, Xena showed up about then to break me out of jail. But of course, as was probably written in stone by the gods, Good Twin and Evil Twin finally confronted each other. And, of course, as was probably written in stone by the same gods, Good Twin and Evil Twin began to fight. We were firmly in Archetype Territory here, and I had to wonder if the gods meant to leave either twin alive and uncursed.

Xena didn't have any such hesitations. She promptly showed that even stories written in stone can be edited— by knocking Evil Twin Jett cold. Cleopatra was saved; Joxer's good-guy reputation was saved.

And as for me, I have decided that if ever a duplicate of me turns up, I am going to have a good, long talk with whatever god is writing the story!

SUCH A PRETTY SHADE
OF GRAY

In the days when I was still living back in my peaceful
village, and even after I first set out to follow Xena, I firmly
believed that the world was divided into black and white,
that is, you were either all evil or all good.

Nonsense, of course. I quickly learned that the truth lies
somewhere in between. That is, we all have some of each
side in us, and the truth is often neither black nor white,
but some pretty shade of gray.

An example:

Surprise, surprise, Ares was mixed up in this one,
stealing metal from the forge of the divine smith, He-
phaestus, so that the mortal warlord Agathon would be
Ares' unstoppable force on earth.

How do you stop the unstoppable? With the unthink-
able. Xena gathered together a small, select group of
prison scum. Useful scum, as it turned out, trained in their
warrior skills by Xena back in her bad old days. In other
words, fight fire with fire: use bad guys to stop bad guys.

Actually, one of them, a man named Darnelle, didn't

seem all that bad. And he and the woman named Glaphyra quarreled so much that anyone could see love—or at least lust—growing between them.

Unfortunately, though, the others were another matter. And, no, you can't trust scum. Sure enough, we were betrayed. But, yes, not all bad guys are bad through and through: Darnelle and Glaphyra came through. With their help, we won, destroying Agathon's precious hoard of metal—something we could never have done if Xena had insisted on using utterly good guys.

Oh, and, yes, Darnelle and Glaphyra decided to go off together to quarrel happily ever after and be at least reasonably good guys.

What about Xena and me? We had a nice heart-to-heart talk. And she gave me one of the loveliest compliments I've received, one that touched me to the heart:

Xena told me that she wouldn't be who she is without me, because I'd been her teacher.

Me? It seems impossible. But . . . well . . . maybe it's true. As true as any pretty shade of gray, anyhow.

Nerves of Steal

And, no, that's not a mistake. I've already mentioned how life is seldom divided into clear black and white, so now I really should write about a fellow who has his feet firmly planted in both camps, and who steals freely from both.

I'm speaking about Autolycus, you see, the self-proclaimed King of Thieves.

Autolycus, I have to admit, is a good-looking guy. The only trouble is, he'd be the first to tell you that. And of course, as a thief, his morals are a bit on the "me first" side.

But Xena and I owe him a great deal. Even though I suspect that, aside from the hope of profit, he wouldn't have chosen to get involved in the first place.

Well . . . *chosen* isn't quite the word.

It was back in the dark days when Xena was . . . when she had . . . when, as far as I knew, Xena had died, and I was taking her body home to Amphipolis. And, yes, she really was dead, then. But . . .

Autolycus probably thought the idea to steal the Dagger of Helios was his own plan. Right. Once he'd stolen that dagger, he found himself . . . inhabited. By Xena. By her spirit, anyhow. I would love to have seen the initial argument between them over whose body it was, and I can only imagine the poor guy's shock when he looked in a pool and saw not him but her!

Anyhow, Autolycus might not have had a choice in the matter, but at the same time I have a strong suspicion that he was perfectly willing to help Xena get that ambrosia. And I don't mean for any purely selfish reasons, either. After all, when Xena asked him to let her speak through him so I'd know what was going on, he didn't really try to argue. And in the few moments when Xena's spirit had transferred into my body, Autolycus could have betrayed us or just run off.

No. He stayed. And I suspect that, deep inside him, in that sentimental good-guy corner I know he has, our King of Thieves really wanted to see things work out right. As, of course, they did, once Xena had tasted the ambrosia.

And as for that certain famous moment: Did I mean to kiss Xena or Autolycus?

That, dear readers, is for you to figure out.

PROSE AND CONS

I'm certainly not advocating setting out to cheat someone. Certainly not.

Not unless that someone really, really deserved it.

After all, what would you call a person who deliberately had the life nearly beaten out of someone as innocent as Joxer? I mean, the poor guy had won perfectly honestly at Titus' establishment, and if he later lost that gold to two charming con men, well, that still wasn't any sort of excuse for Titus to nearly kill him!

What do you do when a friend is so viciously wronged? Call the authorities in on the wrongdoer? What if the wrongdoer is wealthy enough or powerful enough to pretty much do what he wants?

No, you don't want to use force, either. That's sinking to his level. Besides, using force gets a lot of innocent bystanders hurt, and neither Xena nor I will stand for that.

So, what *do* you do?

Simple! You con two con men into working a con on the guy who couldn't work a con on Joxer and had him beaten up instead.

Enough "cons" in there?

Not yet.

One con man, Rafe, bet the other con man, Eldon, that he could con Xena into kissing him. But Rafe conned himself by revealing a soft side, caring about the injured Joxer. Or was that a con, too? Xena wasn't sure. But I was sure about something: she was attracted to him.

Anyhow, the next series of cons: Xena and I conned Titus' favorite ruby from him. Eldon conned Titus into believing Eldon had betrayed us. Rafe conned Titus into thinking that Eldon had killed Rafe. Xena conned Titus but good at the card table. The upshot: the con worked.

But there's still a couple to go: Rafe conned Eldon into believing that Xena's kissing Rafe was a con, losing Eldon the wager. And Xena and Rafe conned themselves into believing there was nothing between them—or at least I think that was a con. And that there was nothing between them.

That's the way it goes with cons. They continue, contentiously. And you never do know the end of them.

WRITE ON

Some people wonder about my stories: how accurate they are, and whether they are of any worth.

About the first question: Hey, I was there! I actually saw Cleopatra and Helen of Troy, and I helped Xena keep the peace between the Amazons and the Centaurs.

As for the second . . . well, I can't very well judge the artistic merit of my own writings, though I think, with no false modesty here, that they're pretty good. But as for their historical worth . . . ah, that's another matter.

Think about it. Without any written records of the time and place, who would know the truth?

Imagine. What if Xena went down in history as a villain, just because no one thought to chronicle her turning to the side of Good and her adventures as a hero? What if, for that matter, no one in later eras knew about her at all?

And Joxer: Suppose by some weird quirk of Fate, all the people of the future had to go on about him was that song he invented, "Joxer the Mighty"? Can you imagine the people of the future believing it was true? Joxer going down in history as a mighty hero?

While we're on the subject of mighty heroes, without an

account to set things straight, no one would ever know how Meleager the Mighty overcame that handicap of drink to regain his position as a genuine hero.

Ha, and what of Autolycus? Granted, he's not exactly a hero, or a good guy, but he's hardly a dark villain, either! Without a scroll to set things right, our dashing King of Thieves would go down in history as a mere robbing hood.

See what I mean? Without written records, we would lose so much.

Including something that I would never, ever want the world to lose. And that is the record of the dear friendship between the bard Gabrielle and Xena, Warrior Princess.

Friendship is, after all, one of the greatest lessons anyone can learn.

Deep Down, Everyone's
a Warrior Princess

Well, isn't that the truth?

Of course, I don't mean we all literally want to be a direct copy of Xena. And maybe not *everyone*. I really wouldn't want to see, say, Joxer dressed up as a warrior woman! Or, for that matter, any other sort of a woman.

But, confess. Don't you, all you women out there, have a sneaking desire for freedom? Think about it. Not having to answer to anyone but yourself, being able to just get out there and kick some . . . ah . . . rumps. Of course you dream about that!

We all have it, you see: the dream of freedom. Or rather, freedom from the mundane world. No more drab lives, no more washing dirty dishes or soothing crying babies. No more letting anyone else boss us around.

Some women take that dream a little bit too far. Look at Minya. Now, Minya is a good, uh, sturdy young woman, quite, shall we say, energetic. But to win her boyfriend back, she dressed up as Xena. As I say, Minya's a fine person in her own right, and I rather like her, but she's not exactly . . . well . . . Xenaesque.

Granted, she had an excuse. Minya, you see, was scared that she was losing her boyfriend, Hower, who'd developed a crush on Xena. Now, imitation may be the sincerest form of flattery, but Minya could easily have done herself—or one of us—permanent damage!

However, that situation worked out happily for everyone concerned. And your own situation can work out happily, too.

Mind you, I am not saying a woman should let anyone boss her around or ever put up with abuse. But there is nothing wrong at all in deciding to be your own person. Not a copy of anyone else—*you*. If that you realizes that she actually likes sleeping under the stars and getting bitten by mosquitoes, that's fine. But if you realize that, by all the gods, you *like* staying home with the husband and youngsters, that's fine, too!

Remember, not every battle takes place on the battlefield, and not every victory is won by the sword. Oh, and remember this, too: nobody ever said that a true Warrior Princess has to actually look like one.

"No one should pass up their dreams."

*Xena, "Athens City Academy
of the Performing Bards"*

Translator's Afterword

Do these scrolls not give us a unique perspective on history, mythology, and the everyday lives of very unusual people?

There are, of course, the skeptics, those who would, out of misguided scholarship, deny the accuracy of the translations. Surely, such skeptics say, the language spoken would be more elegant and refined. To this, the translator retorts, Never! Let it be said with no false modesty that, after considerable effort and study, this translator can indeed claim to be as close to the contents of these scrolls as Gabrielle herself!

But that calls up another topic for the skeptics. Some deny the attribution of the scrolls' contents to Gabrielle. Surely, these misguided souls say, a young woman from so provincial a town as Poteidaia could never have expressed such wisdom, such insights into human and, yes, divine nature. I point out that other skeptics have tried and failed to prove that the works of Shakespeare were written by another! If these are not the true words of Gabrielle, then she and Xena never truly existed!

Are there more scrolls yet to be translated? Very possibly; the excavations will continue for another season, at least. There have even been rumors of finds of similar scrolls, these bearing the words "Adventures of Hercules."

But that, as Gabrielle herself might say, is another story.

30172791R00083

Made in the USA
Lexington, KY
07 February 2019